POETRY A-Z with Mr. E.

Written by: Ebria Keiffer II

POETRY A-Z with Mr. E.

Written by: Ebria Keiffer II
Illustrations by: Elena Yalcin

Copyright © 2021 by Mystical Publishing

Ordering Information:
For details, contact mysticalpublishing11@gmail.com
Printed in the United States of America on SFI Certified paper.

First Edition

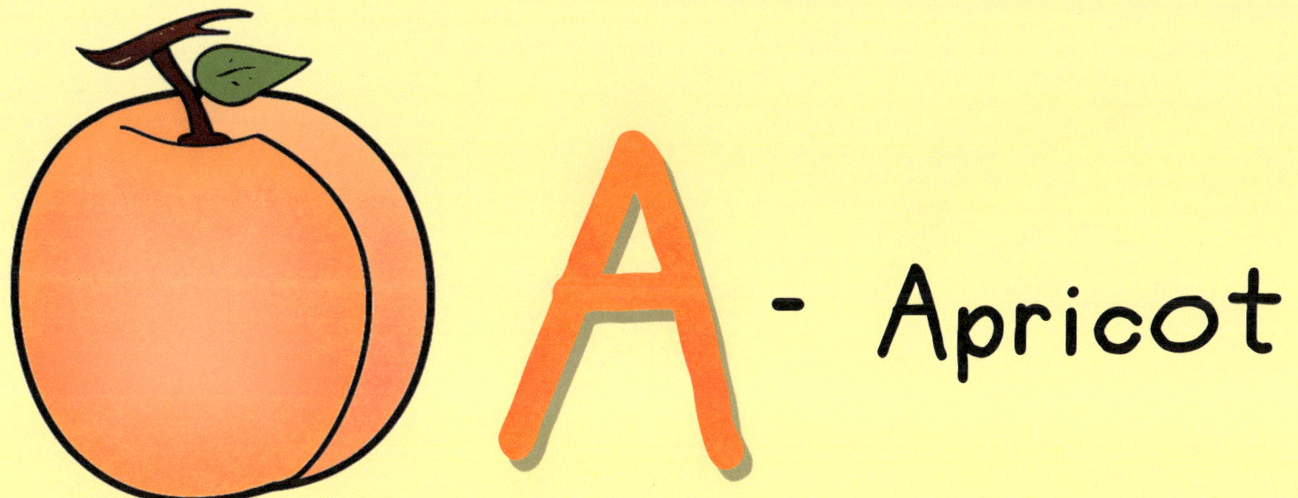

Apricots are round,
So when they roll,
You don't hear a
Sound;

If apricots
Were square would
They taste like
A pear;

If apricots could taste like mangoes,
Would they go to Spain to do the tango,
Would apricots be easy to see if they were
Tall like a fig tree;

If apricots could be combined with metal,
Would they be able to bend like a pedal
If apricots were small could they roll
Like a small ball;

Man, how I love my small blue ball,
It is not the tallest ball, but it is the best
Ball and I love my very own small blue kind of
Ball;

It fits me fine, and that is so divine,
Because my small blue ball can bounce,
Off of many walls, it is my favorite tiny,
Blue ball;

I love to watch my small blue ball,
Roll and bounce all over the place,
You know I love my small blue ball,
Cause there is nothing like mine;

My ball is so unique I could never have another,
This ball right here is special, I will never want another,
This ball is one that no one can call upon because
This ball is my favorite ball.

C - Cat

Who wants to see my new cat,
So for those who don't know him,
His name is Matt, and he is a fat cat,
When I say he is fat, I mean he is super fat;

Sometimes I forget Matt is a cat, and I mistakenly,
Call him a fat rat; this always happens because he is,
A super fat cat, why is Matt a fat cat,
Matt, why are you so big!

I love Matt because the first time I bought Matt,
I told him to sit,
He sat, this is why I love my fat cat Matt;

If I had to give away my fat cat Matt,
I would have to say no way,
Because Matt is my favorite cat,
And that is that!

D - Dog

Not only do I have a fat cat named Matt,
But Not only do I have a fat cat named matt,
But I have a dog named Clog,
He's not fat but slim,
Sort of like a Slim Jim;

One thing about Clog is that,
He likes to sit on a log,
So basically I call him,
Clog the dog on a log;

Not only that,
But Clog sometimes,
Eats like a hog,
He also gets scared like a little,
Frog;

Now my dog Clog is a dog on a log,
Who likes to eat like a hog,
That acts like a frog,
That boy Clog is my favorite dog.

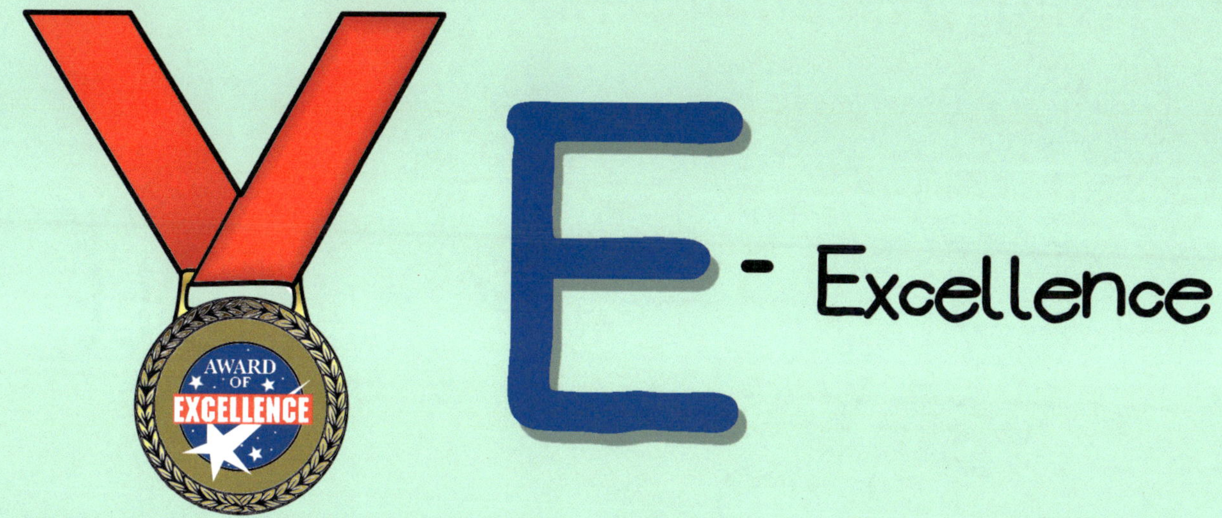

Do you know what our parents expect out of us,
Not Do you know what our parents expect out of us,
Not to be rich or famous,
But they expect excellence,
Here's why;

When a person has excellence,
It is the thing that will take you far,
It opens specific windows,
Such as;

It can open jobs, college choices,
And can even help you become rich,
But all of this requires excellence,
If you want it;

Then you'll be able to get these choices,
But, as I said,
It requires all requires excellence,
So don't be average, have distinction;

One of the things I hate the most is too,
Fall, One of the things I hate the most is too,
Fall, I always thought it was better,
To crawl instead,
To walk;

The tricky thing about a person and,
Falling is that,
When there is no one around,
It is hard for you to find someone to call;

When you fall, don't cry,
Just try to get back up,
It won't hurt to,
Wipe off the dirt,

When your friend,
Asks to say it was you,
Who did that wrongdoing,
Don't say yes and tell them,
You take the fall.

G - Good

Everything is better than bad,
The one thing that makes it bad,
At the bottom of the list is,
Good;

When a person is good,
People want to be your friend and,
Hang out with you,
On the other hand,

When a person is bad,
Then people will think you are,
A person that likes to be mad,
And believe you are being bad for attention,

Here's what I think,
Be great instead of trying to,
Be so filled with hate,
Be yourself instead of being an imposter.

Aw,
The sweet taste of honey,
The only thing is that,
It looks kind of funny,

The only thing sweeter than honey,
Is probably a cute little bunny,
What is lovely about honey,
Is that;

Honey has a sweet taste,
That;

D
R
I
P
S;

Down your chin like a sweet,
And successful win;

I - Ice

Ice is one thing that is cold on,
My tongue,
But the weird thing is,
It is only frozen water;

Why is this thing so

C
O
L
D;

It tastes good on hot days,
The best day to eat it is
In may,
You know this thing I'm talking about,
Its ice!

J - Jump

I love to jump,
Everywhere I go,
Nothing compares,
To me liking to;

Jump,
Not even the biggest

B
U
M
P;

Can't stop me from doing,
What I love best,
And that is jumping,
Here's why;

I love jumping,
I think it is the best exercise in the world!

K - Kool Aid

I see,
Nothing but a big carton,
Of red powder,
With a lemonade jug, man;

The jug man,
Is holding some red like juice,
It looks like it can slip down,
My throat;

Like rushing water,
From Niagara Falls,
It slowly finds its path,
Down to my stomach;

And the reaction of it all is,
Is,
Ah,
As you taste that cool and refreshing
Kool-Aid.

Isn't it amazing,
How people aren't,
Appreciative for two,
Legs;

But that is not always true,
Some people would instead trade,
Their leg,
Just to eat an egg;

In fact,
I know a guy named Greg,
Who would instead trade his leg,
For one little egg;

But that does not make a lot of sense,
Because I love my two legs,
I would not beg for better legs,
No way;

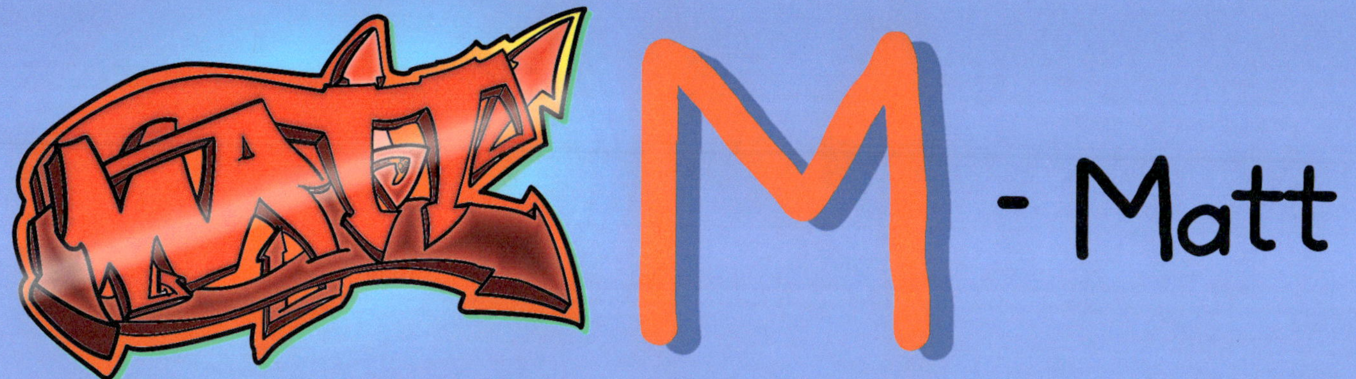

M - Matt

I wanna tell you,
I want to tell you,
About a guy named Matt,
He lived in an apartment,
With his cat;

This cat played with his toy,
A stuffed bat,
Which this toy was super fat,
While he was playing with this fat toy bat;

Mr. Matt was scared of giant fats rats,
And he saw one on his mat,
This he knew,
For a fact;

Poor Mr. Matt,
Who had a cat with a fat toy bat,
Who was scared of fat rats,
I guess that was that.

NATE N - Nate

O,
Mr. Nate, who had already eaten,
Had went outside to play,
And while Mr. Nate was out to play,

He met a girl named Kate,
He could not wait to talk to,
Her,
And he said;

O,
Ms. Kate,
My name is Nate,
Want to get a plate,
So Kate said;

Sorry, Nate,
I don't eat regular food,
My favorite food is bate,
So instead, they went to the park to skate.

O - Oreo

Two chocolate cookies with icing smack,
In the middle of each cookie,
But the temptation of it is,
That it is the best cookie;

And the best part I think is,
That is a cookie that rhymes with,
The word,
Rio;

It used to be a breakfast cereal,
But,
Now it is just a plain old,
Cookie;

Now, this cookie is hard to come by.
It is not a Creole creation,
But an idea went big,
This cookie is the Oreo, my friend.

P - Pen

My wonderful pen can do many things,
It can change ink color with one click,
It has a cap, or it can click,
My pen is so smart;

It can turn into my friend Ben,
Since my pen is so smart,
From a scale of 1 to 10,
My pen is a perfect 10;

My pen is a perfect truly,
But, it is kind of an actual rule,
To have a pen this cool,
I love my pen;

When you use a pen don't abuse it,
Love it, pens will always be pens,
So be respectful of your
Pen;

Q - Quilt

O your majesty,
How I just love your quilt,
Do you know this quilt was handmade just for you,

I had this unique quilt made for you in New Orleans,
I hope you love it,
It is a good quilt;

Do you love,
It was specially built just for you,
Hope you are in love,
You must like it;

It is so
      L
      O
      N
      G;

It is so unique. I hope you love it.

Do you know what my favorite exercise is,
Well if you don't,
It is running,
I just love running;

When my family takes a run,
We always have tons of fun,
When I am done with my run I eat
A honey bun for completing my fun run;

When my god sister takes a run,
She always makes sure her bun is done,
During her run,
We just love to run;

When you have nothing to do,
Take a run,
It is just tons of fun,
Just try a run, for fun;

S - Sun

Man,
It is so hot today,
It feels like summer in winter,
Its just so hot;

The sun is bringing so much heat,
There is not enough time to make my clean beat,
New Orleans why are you so hot,
That my hair rolls into a knot;

Does the sun bring rays of long heat,
Or does it bring a sign of,
Fake sleet,
It is just unpredictable,

Either way the sun is a hot bowl of fun,
It is cool to play in the sun,
I did not know it was that much fun,
Man, Thank you sun;

T - Tall

Do you remember my cat, Matt,
Well, he is not just fat,
But he can walk like a human,
Weird trait for a fat cat;

He stands tall,
Like a 2 foot wall,
That is how tall,
He is,

He slowly falls,
But that is not all,
He can be as tall,
As an ant bed,

I love my cat that has
His feet flat,
He is one
Good tall flat cat;

U - Umbrella

Man, how my sister just loves,
Her umbrella, she never goes,
Anywhere without that umbrella,
Because that umbrella is her Cinderella;

She dreams that it is,
As tall as my brother's rocket,
Who has one small socket,
she loves it that much,

Her mind and that umbrella,
Work like two brain cells,
Working together to answer a question,
Yea, that love;

Her umbrella has never walked away from her side,
It is a little kid with his mom,
Never leaves her side,
That much love for her umbrella;

V - Violin

I love to play my violin,
Oh how it makes its many different sighs,
It makes many types of noises like that makes me,
Warm inside;

My violin can make sounds like,
SCREECH;

Man I just love to play my violin,
It makes me warm inside;

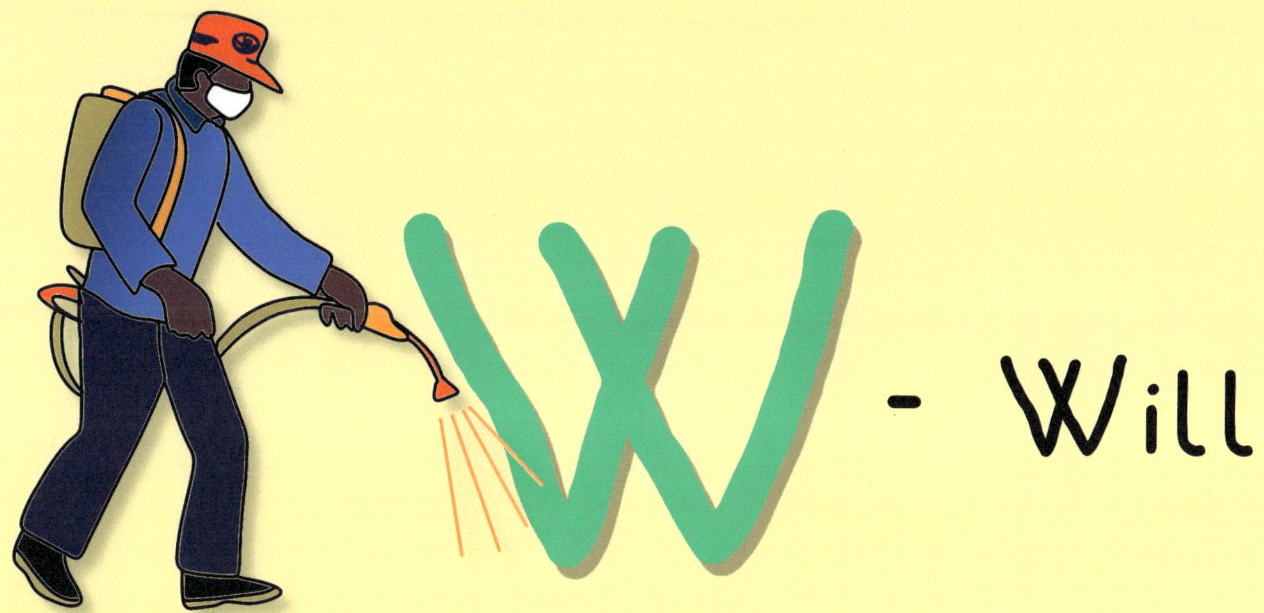

W - Will

Everyone meet my cousin Will,
His job is to collect a certain bill,
Also his job is to exterminate or kill Bugs;

To me,
Will is super cool,
Because he has two jobs,
With collecting bills and killing
Bugs;

I just love Will,
He is a person
Who can collect a bill,
And make a big kill;

X - X-ray

Your body runs through the X-ray machine,
You hear beeps,
And when you're done, you hear one more beep.
X-rays will help you stay healed and safe,
Without an X-ray, how will you know you're ok?!

Y- Yellow Yak

Meet Yugi the Yellow Yak.
He is not your average Yellow Yak,
As Yugi does not like to move in a pack.
Even though Yugi is a nice Yak,
Do not mess with him, or he will have you screaming,
Help Yugi the Yellow Yak is trying to Attack!

Z - Zebra

How can an animal have this many stripes,
It is crazy how all of his stripes are just black and white,
Although he kind of looks like a horse,
And his Zodiac sign is a libra,
He's your favorite striped animal,
A zebra!

Made in the USA
Monee, IL
07 July 2026

56550981R00019